HARLEM HELLFIGHTERS

Essential Library

An Imprint of Abdo Publishing
abdopublishing.com

ESSENTIAL LIBRARY OF
WORLD WAR I

BY SHANNON BAKER MOORE

CONTENT CONSULTANT

JUSTIN QUINN OLMSTEAD, PHD
ASSISTANT PROFESSOR OF HISTORY
UNIVERSITY OF CENTRAL OKLAHOMA

abdopublishing.com

Published by Abdo Publishing, a division of ABDO, PO Box 398166, Minneapolis, Minnesota 55439. Copyright © 2016 by Abdo Consulting Group, Inc. International copyrights reserved in all countries. No part of this book may be reproduced in any form without written permission from the publisher. Essential Library™ is a trademark and logo of Abdo Publishing.

Printed in the United States of America, North Mankato, Minnesota

092015
012016

THIS BOOK CONTAINS
RECYCLED MATERIALS

Cover Photo: US National Archives and Records Administration
Interior Photos: US National Archives and Records Administration, 1; International Film Service/US National Archives and Records Administration, 4, 62, 98 (bottom), 99 (top); AP Images, 8; Private Needham Roberts, 10; US Army/AP Images, 11; Paul Thompson/US National Archives and Records Administration, 12; Library of Congress, 14, 19, 21; Corbis, 17; Everett Historical/Shutterstock Images, 24, 29, 32, 48, 91, 98 (top); Public Domain, 27, 72; Underwood Archives/UIG Universal Images Group/Newscom, 34, 68; Bain News Service/Library of Congress, 37, 57; Harvard Theatre Collection/Houghton Library/Harvard University, 39; Underwood & Underwood/US National Archives and Records Administration, 41, 64, 83, 86; John Gomez/Shutterstock Images, 43; Stapleton Historical Collection/Heritage Images/Glow Images, 45; Historic American Buildings Survey/Library of Congress, 51; Bettmann/Corbis, 53; akg-images/Newscom, 58; US Naval Historical Center, 60; Red Line Editorial, 70; Imperial War Museum, 76; US Marines/US National Archives and Records Administration, 78; Western Newspaper Union/US National Archives and Records Administration, 80, 84, 88, 99 (bottom); University of Washington, 93; New York World-Telegram and the Sun Newspaper Photograph Collection Library of Congress, 95

Editor: Jenna Gleisner
Series Designers: Kelsey Oseid and Maggie Villaume

Library of Congress Control Number: 2015945637

Cataloging-in-Publication Data

Moore, Shannon Baker.
 Harlem Hellfighters / Shannon Baker Moore.
  p. cm. -- (Essential library of World War I)
 ISBN 978-1-62403-922-5 (lib. bdg.)
 Includes bibliographical references and index.
 1. United States.Army.Infantry Regiment, 369th--Juvenile literature. 2. World War, 1914-1918--Participation, African American--Juvenile literature. 3. United States.Army--African American troops--History--20th century--Juvenile literature. 4. African American soldiers--History--20th century--Juvenile literature.   I. Title.
 940.54/03--dc23
                                                                    2015945637

CONTENTS

Privates Henry Johnson, *left*, and Needham Roberts, *right*, single-handedly defeated German troops on the night of May 15, 1918.

BATTLING BLACK DEATH

It was midnight, and Private Henry Johnson sat in the dark listening for the enemy. It was a moonlit night—easier for spotting the enemy, but also easier for getting spotted. Every sound seemed magnified in the darkness. Private Johnson, along with fellow soldier Private Needham Roberts, had volunteered for the midnight to 4:00 a.m. patrol of Outpost 29, an isolated listening post that was part of the French defenses against enemy German forces.

Although Johnson and Roberts weren't French, their unit—the 369th US Infantry—was among the first of US troops sent to help fight in the Great War in Europe, the war that became known as World War I (1914–1918). On the night of May 15, 1918, Johnson and Roberts had one mission: listen for any signs of the enemy and report the news so the front line could prepare for attack.

The listening post wasn't much protection—just a hole in the ground with some planks for a floor, surrounded by tall grass and barbed wire. Roughly 50 yards (46 m) behind Outpost 29 was Post 28 and the rest of Johnson's patrol. Fifty yards (46 m) behind that was the main trench, where the rest of the troops were restlessly sleeping.

TRENCH WARFARE

Trench warfare is combat during which troops fight from trenches, or deep ditches. Thousands of miles of trenches were dug during World War I. The trench system consisted of three rows of parallel ditches. The first row was the front line for fighting. The second row, which was approximately 3.5 to 5 miles (5.6 to 8 km) behind the front line, was another trench for reserve troops. The third row, approximately 5 to 7.5 miles (8 to 12 km) behind the support line, was a service line, wide enough to fit supply trucks and ambulances. Communication trenches ran perpendicularly between the three main trenches to connect them. To reduce damage from attack, trenches were not built in straight lines. Instead, they zigzagged.

Johnson tensed in the darkness, alert to any possible enemy movement. At approximately 1:00 a.m., a sniper fired at Johnson. Soon came more enemy fire. Figuring he'd better get ready for an attack, Johnson laid out a row of roughly 30 hand grenades.

He didn't have long to wait. Approximately an hour later, Johnson heard the snip of wire cutters. The Germans were clipping through the barbed wire defenses. Johnson called to Roberts and told him to leave and go warn the lieutenant.

The snipping sound came again, this time closer. Johnson threw a hand grenade.

The enemy opened fire and charged. Germans were everywhere—at least 28 of them. Roberts raced back toward the outpost to help Johnson but was hit by a grenade. Unable to walk or use his arm, Roberts lay on the floor and handed Johnson grenades. Johnson felt shots clip him, but he kept fighting. He lobbed grenade after grenade and then opened fire with his rifle. One of his three shots killed an enemy soldier, but then Johnson's French rifle jammed after he accidentally reloaded it with American ammunition.

His gun now useless, Johnson turned it into a club and started swinging. As the Germans tried dragging Roberts away as a prisoner, Johnson smashed the butt of his rifle into the enemy. He swung so hard the handle shattered. With only one weapon left, a nine-inch (23-cm) knife, Johnson fought on. Johnson received multiple injuries, but he got in one last fatal blow as he slashed at the German preparing to kill him. Suddenly, the Germans heard the sound of Johnson's reinforcements and fled. Sinking to the ground with a total of 21 wounds, Johnson lobbed a final grenade and passed out.

THE MAJOR POWERS OF WORLD WAR I

World War I began in Europe, and gradually countries joined together into two main groups: the Central powers and the Entente powers (also called the Allies). The main countries of the Central powers were Germany, Austria-Hungary, and the Ottoman Empire. The main Allied countries were the United Kingdom, France, and Russia, with the United States joining in 1917. Because the European countries had colonies and international agreements, World War I eventually spread around the globe and included roughly 30 countries.

As trenches were separated by no-man's-land and protected with barbed wire, soldiers often cut through the wire quietly in pursuit of the enemy.

WAR HEROES

Johnson and Roberts survived the attack and immediately became war heroes.

Their stunning victory against the Germans grew even more legendary when

Major Arthur Little investigated the combat site the next day. A trail of blood easily showed where the Germans had fled. Major Little found a variety of enemy equipment, including bandages, torn clothing, 40 enemy grenades, three automatic pistols, and seven wire cutters. This evidence, plus the fact that the Germans issued one wire cutter for every four men, led Little to conclude Johnson had single-handedly defeated at least 28 men. Some officials thought the number might be as high as 40.[1] The story quickly spread as US reporters wired the news back to the states. Former president Theodore Roosevelt said Johnson was one of the "five bravest Americans" to serve in World War I.[2]

In recognition of such bravery, the French government awarded Johnson and Roberts the Croix de Guerre, France's highest military honor. These soldiers were the first two Americans ever to receive such an honor, and Johnson's medal included the Gold Palm, an even more prestigious award given for extraordinary valor, or courage. The entire French force fighting in the area lined up for the award

YOUNG BLACK JOE

White writer Irvin S. Cobb helped spread the tale of Johnson's stunning battle. Published on August 24, 1918, Cobb's story "Young Black Joe" appeared in popular magazine the *Saturday Evening Post*. A southern writer, Cobb had a reputation for portraying blacks in racist terms. Nevertheless, in "Young Black Joe," Cobb praised the black regiment: "They were soldiers who wore their uniforms with a smartened pride; who were jaunty and alert and prompt in their movements; and who expressed . . . a sincere heartfelt inclination to get a whack at the foe."[3] Cobb's story brought Johnson national media attention and was widely reprinted in black papers.

Johnson proudly wears his Croix de Guerre medal.

ceremony. Ultimately Johnson and Roberts' entire unit—171 officers and men—were awarded the Croix de Guerre for their 191 days of continuous service on the war front—a record for US forces in World War I.

THE FIFTEENTH NEW YORK NATIONAL GUARD

Johnson and Roberts were two of the nearly 380,000 African Americans who served in World War I.[4] They were part of an all-black unit made up of men primarily from New York, particularly Harlem. The unit was created as the Fifteenth New York National Guard and renamed the 369th US Infantry when it joined with the French Fourth Army to fight in France. But the unit's

HENRY JOHNSON

1897–1929

Nicknamed Black Death, Henry Lincoln Johnson was born in 1897 in Alexandria, Virginia. Johnson left home as a teenager, ultimately getting a job as a porter at Union Station in Albany, New York. On June 5, 1917, he enlisted in the Fifteenth New York National Guard. After fighting off a German attack on May 15, 1918, Johnson and fellow soldier Needham Roberts were awarded the Croix de Guerre, France's highest military honor. They were the first two Americans ever to receive such an honor. Johnson was promoted to sergeant just before his release from the army.

After the war, Johnson gave promotional speeches for the army, but the long-term physical and emotional effects of the war took their toll. His injuries made him unable to return to his work, but because his paperwork hadn't recorded his injuries, he was given neither disability pay nor a Purple Heart medal. Johnson died in 1929 at age 32.

In 1996, President Bill Clinton awarded Johnson the Purple Heart. The US Army awarded Johnson the Distinguished Service Cross for bravery in 2003. On June 2, 2015, President Barack Obama awarded Johnson the Congressional Medal of Honor, the country's top award for bravery, 97 years after Johnson earned it.

Members of the 369th US Infantry celebrate as they return home from war in February 1919.

most famous name is the nickname the German troops gave them: the Harlem Hellfighters, a name they earned for their ferocious skill on the battlefield. The Harlem Hellfighters never lost a foot of ground and never had a man taken prisoner. They did, however, lose 200 men who gave their lives on the battlefields of France during World War I, and the unit suffered 1,500 casualties (wounded or killed).[5]

As for Johnson, although small in size—only 5 feet 4 inches (163 cm) tall and 130 pounds (60 kg)—his big battle earned him the nickname Black Death. This bloody battle, however, was part of a much bigger struggle: the fight against racism. For Johnson, Roberts, and all the Harlem Hellfighters, their victories were in France, but their biggest fight raged on in the states—the battle for racial equality and equal justice under the law.

Beginning in the 1600s, slaves were sold to plantation owners after being transported to America against their will.

THE FIGHT FOR FREEDOM

African Americans have fought in every major US conflict since the Revolutionary War (1775–1783). Their history in the United States has been a legacy of fighting for freedom. The first Africans, approximately 20 people, arrived in colonial Virginia in 1619.[1] According to historical records, these Africans were not slaves but indentured servants, meaning they had agreed to work for three to five years in exchange for free ocean crossing, food, and housing. Most Africans, however, came to the American colonies as slaves. The first Boston, Massachusetts, slaves arrived in 1638. Slaves were found throughout the American colonies, but the soil and climate of the southern colonies were better for large-scale farming. Plantation agriculture required vast amounts of labor, and slavery grew as cheap labor was needed for crops such as tobacco. In time, the South became more dependent on slaves as an important part of its economy. In the 1750s, almost 90 percent of the 242,000 slaves in North America lived in Maryland, Virginia, and the southern colonies.[2]

THE AMERICAN REVOLUTION

African Americans played a significant role in the Revolutionary War. The first colonist killed by British troops during the Boston Massacre on March 5, 1770, was a free black man named Crispus Attucks. Black men fought in the early battles of the revolution, at Lexington and Concord, Ticonderoga, and Bunker Hill. But despite their loyal service, the Continental Congress banned blacks from joining the military. Meanwhile, the British offered freedom to black slaves who joined the British. Blacks hoped the revolution would lead to freedom for black slaves, but many were skeptical of white Revolutionary leaders. After all, 14 of the 21 signers of the Declaration of Independence owned slaves.

Initially, General George Washington was opposed to black soldiers, but in 1775, he asked Congress to allow free blacks to enlist. Roughly 5,000 African Americans fought for the American colonies during the Revolutionary War.[3] The First Rhode Island Regiment, a unit that was more than half black, fought at the

African Americans, including Crispus Attucks, *center*, fought for freedom alongside American colonists during the Revolutionary War.

battle of Yorktown in 1781, which led to the surrender of the British and the end of the war.

Some slaves gained their freedom as a result of the Revolutionary War, but most did not. The Declaration of Independence claimed all men were created equal and that liberty and freedom were inalienable rights nobody could strip of another human, yet in 1790, there were 698,000 slaves in the United States.[4] When colonial leaders met to craft the Constitution, they hotly debated the slavery issue, but in the end, the northern and southern colonies compromised. The US Constitution, which the states approved in 1788, protected slavery.

Sometimes leaders justified their views by claiming blacks were simply inferior to whites and so were not entitled to the same freedoms.

INTERNAL CONFLICT

At times, African Americans felt torn between loyalty to their country and loyalty to their race. Many loved their country, yet they felt their country didn't love them. They protected their country, yet their country wouldn't protect them. As writer and civil rights activist W. E. B. (William Edward Burghardt) Du Bois said, "It is a peculiar sensation. . . . One ever feels his twoness,—an American, a Negro; two souls, two thoughts, two unreconciled strivings; two warring ideals in one dark body, whose dogged strength alone keeps it from being torn asunder."[5]

AFTER THE REVOLUTION

After the Revolutionary War, other major conflicts arose as the newly formed United States of America sought to maintain and gain additional territory. Once again, African Americans fought for their country. During the War of 1812, black sailors were on every ship that fought during the war, and the courage and daring of some of these black seamen became legendary. African Americans also fought under the command of General Andrew Jackson during the battle of New Orleans. This battle was

White and African-American soldiers fought together in the battle of New Orleans.

the final major conflict of the War of 1812, and two volunteer African-American battalions helped stop the invading British.

Approximately 1,000 African Americans also served in the naval blockade of Mexico during the Mexican-American War (1846–1848).[6] The navy continued recruiting African Americans, but many southern whites opposed black military service. The army allowed blacks to serve only as personal servants.

CIVIL WAR ERA

Just before the Civil War (1861–1865), the black population of the United States was 4,441,830. Almost 4 million of these people were enslaved.[7] When the Civil War began in 1861, thousands of slaves fled north. In 1863, President Abraham Lincoln issued the Emancipation Proclamation, officially freeing slaves in the Confederacy. African Americans, both those who were slaves and those who were free, volunteered to fight for both sides. Well-known African-American leaders such as Frederick Douglass and Martin Robison Delany also urged blacks to enlist. During the war, approximately 180,000 black soldiers fought for the Union in 449 battles, including 39 major battles.[8] There were 140 black regiments. But African-American soldiers faced unfair treatment by the very government they were sacrificing for. For example, the Fifty-Fourth Massachusetts Infantry, an all-black unit, not only fought Confederate soldiers but also fought to receive the same

FREDERICK DOUGLASS (1818–1895)

Frederick Douglass was the most famous African American of the 1800s. Born into slavery on a Maryland plantation, Frederick Augustus Washington Bailey escaped when he was 20. He changed his last name to Douglass and became a famous abolitionist who fought against slavery. A popular speaker, author, and reformer, Douglass wrote three autobiographies. His most famous, *Narrative of the Life of Frederick Douglass, an American Slave, Written by Himself*, was published in 1845. A self-made man, Douglass rose from slavery to become a trusted adviser to President Lincoln.

After President Lincoln, *left*, issued the Emancipation Proclamation, many African Americans chose to fight in the Civil War.

combat pay as white soldiers. They felt the tug of patriotism and duty, yet also the pull of sorrow, anger, and resentment at the unfair treatment they received from their countrymen and government.

After the Civil War, the number of African-American units decreased. However, by this point, the US Army was providing African Americans with equal pay, housing, food, uniforms, horses, and weapons. As a result, many African Americans saw the army as a good career choice that would offer them a fair chance at success. After the Civil War ended in 1865, black troops, sometimes nicknamed Buffalo Soldiers, continued working for the army by patrolling the US-Mexico border, fighting against Native Americans, and occupying the defeated Southern states.

There was widespread racism at the time, particularly in the Southern United States. In 1868, the Fourteenth Amendment granted citizenship to African Americans. In 1870, the Fifteenth Amendment gave African-American men the right to vote. But when Union troops finally left the South in 1877, Southern whites lashed out against African Americans. Southern governments found ways to prevent African Americans from

A CIVIL WAR FIGHT FOR EQUAL PAY

The Fifty-Fourth Massachusetts Infantry Regiment was an all-black unit created in 1863. African Americans served in this unit, including two sons of Frederick Douglass. Promised the same pay as white troops, $13 per month, the Fifty-Fourth arrived for duty only to discover their pay would be only $10 per month because black soldiers were considered laborers. Their colonel, white abolitionist Robert Gould Shaw, demanded equal pay, and the entire regiment refused to accept any pay at all unless it was fair. More than a year later, on June 15, 1864, Congress finally granted equal pay. In September 1864, the men finally received their wages. This regiment was famed for its courage. Almost half of its men were killed or wounded in battle.

voting, and the unfair laws and abuse from whites continued. Slavery may have ended, but the promise of freedom was far from fulfilled.

BUFFALO SOLDIERS

After the Civil War, Congress kept six regiments for black enlisted men—the first time black units were included as a regular part of the army. These units served mainly in the western frontier and got the nickname Buffalo Soldiers around 1870. This nickname supposedly came from Cheyenne Indians who compared the African-American troops' curly hair and dark skin to that of buffalo. At the time, black troops did not use the nickname and didn't like it because army staff used the term as an insult. These regiments also fought in the Spanish-American War (1898), the Philippine Insurrection (1899–1902), and border skirmishes between the United States and Mexico.

Even after they were freed, many African Americans lived in poverty, working as sharecroppers for white farmers.

CHAPTER
★ **3** ★

FIGHTING FOR EQUALITY ON THE HOME FRONT

After the Civil War, blacks continued working for racial equality. Racism was worse in the South, and in the 1890s, nine out of ten black Americans still lived in the South.[1] Beginning around 1915, African Americans began moving north and west, hoping for greater freedom and opportunity. Factories were supplying the war effort in Europe, and they needed more workers. This rising need occurred during a period of ongoing economic, social, and political problems for African Americans.

Economically, most southern blacks still lived in poverty as sharecroppers. Sharecroppers farmed land owned by others (almost always whites), and life was often not much better than slavery. To make matters worse, an insect infestation of boll weevils destroyed much of the cotton crop from 1915 to 1916, also diminishing profits.

JIM CROW LAWS

The term *Jim Crow* refers to laws and practices that discriminated against African Americans and enforced racial segregation. Jim Crow laws were passed primarily in the South from 1876 until around 1960. Scholars think the term *Jim Crow* comes from a white actor named Thomas Dartmouth Rice, who, in the 1820s, played the part of an old black slave named Jim Crow. Jim Crow laws denied African Americans jobs, housing, and other opportunities because of their race. "Whites only" and "colored" signs hung from separate entrances to public buildings, drinking fountains, bathrooms, and elevators. Florida schools even segregated their books; during the summer, books from black schools and white schools had to be stored in separate buildings.

LYNCHING AND SEGREGATION

Segregation laws, often called Jim Crow laws, and lynchings were also a horrible reality for blacks. When blacks were lynched, they were killed illegally, usually from mob violence and usually by hanging. In 1898 alone, there were 101 reported lynchings of African Americans. In most cases, these victims had not been convicted of, or even charged with, a crime. Lynching was cold-blooded murder, and black men knew they might be lynched at any time for any reason. Between 1882 and 1930, 3,386 lynchings were reported, and historians assume many lynchings went

Lynchings were more common in the South, but there were lynchings in the North as well, such as this one in Duluth, Minnesota.

unreported. During World War I, the number of lynchings in the United States rose from 36 in 1917, to 60 in 1918, to 76 in 1919 (the year the troops came home).[2]

Sometimes black men were lynched for trying to vote. Although the Fourteenth and Fifteenth Amendments had granted citizenship to blacks and voting rights to black men, many African Americans were disenfranchised, or deprived of the legal right to vote. When black men went to vote, they were often told they had to be able to read in order to vote, or that they had to pay a fee (which they usually couldn't afford), or they were threatened. Trying to vote often meant risking one's life.

Jim Crow laws created further unfair treatment. For example, African Americans could not attend white schools, use "whites only" bathrooms, or drink from "whites only" drinking fountains. There were laws that segregated elevators, swimming pools, and even telephone booths. The 1896 Supreme Court case known as *Plessy v. Ferguson* upheld segregation as legal. It stated facilities could be separate as long as they provided equal quality for whites and blacks. The reality was that black facilities were far inferior. The military was segregated as well, and officers were almost always white.

The injustices of the South, combined with the rising job market in the North, caused thousands of blacks to migrate

PLESSY V. FERGUSON

Plessy v. Ferguson was a famous Supreme Court case that legalized racial segregation in the United States. In 1890, Louisiana passed a separate-car law that required railroad companies to have separate seating for black and white passengers. On June 7, 1892, Homer Adolph Plessy, a light-skinned black man, bought a first-class ticket and sat in a "whites-only" car. When the conductor ordered Plessy to leave, he refused and was arrested. Plessy's case was tried in court by Judge John H. Ferguson, who ruled the separate-car law was constitutional. Plessy appealed his case to the US Supreme Court, which upheld the Louisiana law. Ultimately, *Plessy v. Ferguson* led to even more drastic segregation laws and racial inequality.

Jim Crow laws even segregated movie theaters, including this one in Leland, Mississippi.

HOME IN HARLEM

As part of the Great Migration, many blacks moved northward and settled in an area of Manhattan, New York, called Harlem. Before the 1900s, almost no blacks lived in Harlem, but by 1916, approximately 50,000 of Manhattan's 60,000 blacks lived there.[4] During the 1920s and 1930s, Harlem became famous for its nightclubs and jazz music, as well as for the Harlem Renaissance, a thriving cultural movement that celebrated African-American art, music, and literature.

northward. This period is called the Great Migration because so many African Americans left the South. From 1890 to 1930, roughly 1.8 million African Americans moved North, with the biggest numbers moving during the World War I era, roughly 500,000 people from 1914 to 1920.[3]

THE GREAT WAR

While World War I was raging in Europe, Americans had plenty of their own problems at home. African Americans, along with Americans in general, saw little reason for getting tangled in Europe's chaos. The war had been sparked on June 28, 1914, when Archduke Franz Ferdinand, heir to the Austro-Hungarian throne, and his wife, Sophia, were assassinated by a Serbian named Gavrilo Princip. In retaliation, Austria-Hungary declared war on Serbia on July 28. By August 29, what had started as a regional conflict was spreading into a world war. Germany sided with Austria-Hungary. Russia sided with Serbia. Germany invaded Luxembourg and Belgium and attacked France. The United Kingdom joined with France and Russia. Meanwhile, the United States tried to stay neutral.

US President Woodrow Wilson won reelection in 1916 with the slogan "He kept us out of war."[5] The war in Europe seemed far off and remote to African Americans who were dealing with segregation, disenfranchisement, racial discrimination, and lynching. African Americans didn't need to go to Europe to fight for freedom—there were plenty of battles to fight at home.

THE FIGHTING FIFTEENTH

Since the early 1900s, African Americans in Harlem, a section of New York City, and other areas had been fighting to be included in the New York National Guard. National Guard units are state-organized military units kept in reserve in case of national or local emergencies. On June 2, 1913, the New York state

WOODROW WILSON AND SEGREGATION

When Woodrow Wilson was elected president in 1912, African Americans were dismayed and shocked by his racial policies. Black leaders had worked for Wilson's election, but Wilson did nothing to address the pressing racial problems that were on the rise. If anything, matters grew worse. During the Wilson administration, government bureaus increased segregation. Agencies such as the Post Office and Census Bureau began segregating offices and restrooms. Blacks were demoted from federal government jobs, and employees who protested were fired. On November 12, 1914, a group of black leaders, led by William Monroe Trotter, met with the president to protest. Trotter and the president got in a shouting match, and President Wilson ordered Trotter from the White House. Trotter then held a press conference on the White House lawn, and as a result, the argument made the front page of the *New York Times*.

President Wilson kept the United States out of much of the war but avoided addressing the issue of segregation in his own country.

legislature officially approved the idea of a Fifteenth New York National Guard regiment, the first African-American National Guard regiment in the state. But nothing happened to make this regiment a reality until 1916, when Governor Whitman announced the formation of a black regiment of the New York National Guard: "You are here, you are part and parcel of America, and there can be no progress in which you are not considered."[6] The man chosen to build the black regiment was a white man by the name of William Hayward.

THE GOVERNOR OKs THE REGIMENT

Both the New York governor, Charles Whitman, and Colonel William Hayward felt African Americans deserved fairer treatment. Although they knew establishing an all-black regiment would present many challenges, both felt African Americans deserved the chance to serve. Colonel Hayward said,

> Governor Whitman was perfectly sincere in his feelings that the great colored population of New York ought to be given an opportunity to shine in the National Guard field without prejudice . . . I felt very deeply on the subject of the negro problem, and the unfairness with which it was being met. When the Governor invited me to accept the designation as Commanding Officer . . . I accepted . . . in all seriousness and in full appreciation of the probable difficulties which lay before me.[7]

Hayward, *right*, would go on to train and lead his Fifteenth National Guard unit in war.

RECRUITING THE FIGHTING FIFTEENTH

Colonel William Hayward, new commanding officer of the Fifteenth New York National Guard Regiment, was a Republican attorney from Nebraska who moved to New York to practice law. He had worked with Governor Whitman in both state government and state politics, serving as the governor's campaign manager during his election campaign. Hayward's close ties to the governor were in large part responsible for his appointment as commanding officer. He had also led African-American troops during the Spanish-American War and was impressed by their bravery.

Hayward also knew that although black leaders wanted a black National Guard unit, they didn't want it run by white men, even though that was what the governor had ordered. One black leader, veteran Charles Fillmore, pushed for the idea of an African-American national guard. Hayward knew he needed not only Fillmore's support but also the support of the black community as a whole if the regiment was to succeed. To have a complete regiment at combat strength, Hayward needed 2,000 men to volunteer.

COLONEL CHARLES YOUNG

During World War I, the highest-ranking black officer in the military was Lieutenant Colonel Charles Young. A West Point graduate and distinguished veteran, many assumed he would lead a black combat division in World War I and become the first African-American general in the United States. Governor Whitman requested that the War Department reassign Young to the Fifteenth. But in July 1917, Colonel Young was retired on medical grounds, a charge Young opposed. Young rode on horseback 500 miles (800 km) from Ohio to Washington, DC, to prove his fitness. Many felt his medical discharge was just an excuse and believed Young was really discharged because of discrimination by white officials who did not want such a high-ranking black officer.

RECRUITMENT BEGINS

Hayward and another white officer, Major Lorillard Spencer, knew one way to encourage men to enlist was to offer them the chance to become officers. Black officers were rare in the US military at the time. Hayward announced that "as rapidly as colored men can and do qualify . . . they will be commissioned as officers."[1] Hayward and Spencer also convinced Vertner Tandy to help with enlistment. Tandy was a well-respected black architect. In June 1916, enlistment began for the Fifteenth New York National Guard Regiment. Hayward printed recruiting

COLONEL WILLIAM HAYWARD

1877–1944

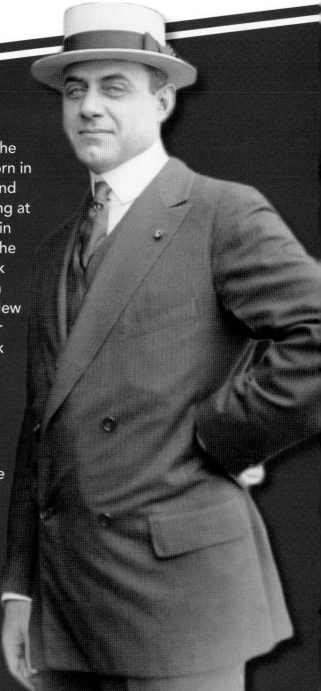

William Hayward was 40 years old when he became colonel of the newly formed New York Fifteenth National Guard Regiment. Born in Nebraska in 1877, Hayward was the son of a Civil War veteran and served as a National Guard cadet under General John J. Pershing at the University of Nebraska. Hayward commanded black troops in the Spanish-American War and eventually became a colonel in the Nebraska National Guard. In 1910, Hayward moved to New York to practice law. He was assistant district attorney and campaign manager for Charles Whitman, who later became governor of New York. Because of Hayward's close ties to Whitman, the governor invited him to be commanding officer of the Fifteenth New York National Guard Regiment.

At a time when many whites questioned the fighting ability of black soldiers, Colonel Hayward said of his men, "There is no better soldier material in the world. Given the proper training, these men will be the equal of any soldiers in the world."[2] Hayward was proud of his men and their role in history: "We are proud to think our boys were the first Negro American soldiers in the trenches. . . . In addition to the personal gratification at having done well as a regiment I feel it has been a tremendously important experiment, when one considers the hosts of colored men who much come after us."[3] Hayward died in 1944 in Manhattan, New York.

posters that announced Tandy was a first lieutenant and would be helping with the recruiting efforts.

The Fifteenth Regiment had little funding and little support, so the first recruiting office was set up in a cigar shop. At one point, the back of a beauty parlor served as headquarters. As enrollment grew, the regiment drilled in theater basements and music halls. They marched in vacant lots and on the streets of Harlem. They didn't have enough uniforms, and they didn't have guns. They paraded around with broomsticks instead.

But Hayward, well-connected and convincing, knew how to get supplies, publicity, and prominent people to help the Fighting Fifteenth. For example, the state quartermaster kept refusing Hayward's request for rifles, but workers at the state arsenal, where firearms were kept, told Hayward there were hundreds of brand-new rifles set aside for civilian shooting clubs. A civilian shooting club was a sports club people could join to practice shooting. So to get the rifles the regiment needed, Hayward had his men start civilian shooting clubs: "Well, I started the darndest set of rifle or civilian shooting clubs that you ever heard of. There was a regular boom. Practically everybody in the regiment in the early days became the president or the secretary of a civilian shooting club, and we put in [an order] and got the rifles delivered to us."[4]

FAMOUS RECRUITS

Several famous black men enlisted in the Fifteenth, and these well-known recruits helped boost enlistment. Spottswood Poles, center fielder for the Negro League's New York Lincoln Giants, was one of Hayward's best-known recruits. Another celebrity enlistee was Bert Williams, a popular vaudeville comedian. Williams had performed comedy acts on Broadway and for the *Ziegfeld Follies* (a popular Broadway show). There was also Napoleon Bonaparte Marshall, a famed Harvard University track star. The Fighting Fifteenth also recruited George "Kid" Cotton, a professional boxer who had sparred with the first black heavyweight champion, Jack Johnson.

Performer Bert Williams enlisted, helping spark more African-American involvement.

JAMES REESE EUROPE AND HIS BAND

The most famous of all Hayward's recruits was the ragtime bandleader James Reese Europe, who enlisted on September 18, 1916. In addition to leading concerts and performing at wealthy high-society parties, Europe directed and composed music for the legendary dance team of Vernon and Irene Castle.

Hayward asked Europe to put together a military band.

The typical regimental band had 28 players, but Europe said that wasn't good enough. According to Hayward, Europe "figured that 44 was the minimum number that a regimental band should have, and that 60-odd would be better."[5] Europe agreed to form a band if Hayward raised $10,000 to pay for the additional musicians. Hayward got the money from a wealthy New York businessman, and Europe went to work forming his band. With James Reese Europe on board as regimental bandleader, other top musicians

RAISING TEN GRAND

The $10,000 James Reese Europe wanted for his regimental band was a huge sum of money in 1916. Colonel Hayward knew he couldn't ask donors for that much. Instead, he went to the millionaire industrialist Daniel G. Reid, nicknamed the Tin Plate King because he had made his fortune in tinplate companies. Hayward asked Reid for letters of introduction to 30 or 40 of Reid's richest contacts. Hayward intended to ask each one for $500. Reid asked how many donations Hayward thought he would actually get. Hayward said about 20. Reid opened his checkbook and wrote out a check for $10,000. He handed it to Hayward, telling him that writing one check was a whole lot easier than writing 40 letters of introduction.

Europe, *left*, created a world-class military band.

from the United States and Puerto Rico signed up as well. Europe and his band were the best advertisement the Fifteenth could ask for.

THE UNITED STATES DECLARES WAR

By 1917, the war had been raging in Europe for three years, but no side had won a decisive victory. Germany had tried to move quickly and crush France before Russia could fully mobilize for war. But this plan had backfired. Russia quickly came to Serbia's aid. German troops got bogged down on the plains near the Belgian border of France. This ground was flat and open with little protection against enemy fire, so troops began digging trenches to defend themselves. Eventually, thousands of miles of trenches were built on both sides. The industrialization of modern war with artillery, machine guns, poison gas, and aerial bombing killed and maimed millions.

The United States had hoped to stay out of the war. But German submarines had been sinking US vessels. A secret telegram known as the Zimmerman telegram also revealed Germany was trying to convince Mexico to join the Central powers if the United States entered the war. One month later, on April 6, 1917, the United States declared war on Germany.

Trenches in Ypres, Belgium, have been preserved.

POISON GAS
DURING WORLD WAR I

As with all troops in World War I, the Harlem Hellfighters knew poison gas was one battle they may have to face in combat. During World War I, approximately 1 million people were killed or injured by poison gases. Developed by scientist Fritz Haber, poison gas was used in 1915 when Germany released 150 short tons (14 metric tons) of chlorine gas across 4.3 miles (6.9 km) within ten minutes. Soldiers began to choke, and 5,000 of these 15,000 gas casualties died.[12]

France developed phosgene gas in 1915, which was 18 times more powerful than chlorine gas. By 1917, the Germans had also developed mustard gas, so called because it smelled like mustard or garlic. The United Kingdom and the United States also used mustard gas.

Depending on the type, poison gas caused blisters, itching, eye irritation, blindness, nausea, vomiting, severe burns, nerve damage, or lung damage. Gas could kill quickly or slowly or cause long-term health problems. It could take hours for someone to develop symptoms from poison gas. Although gas masks helped protect soldiers, masks couldn't be made quickly enough for hundreds of thousands of soldiers. There was no other protective clothing. By the end of World War I, all the major powers had chemical warfare programs.

Temporarily blinded poison victims lead one another at a French hospital.

BLACK OPINION

African Americans had divided views about the war. Many blacks felt the United States was hypocritical to talk about democracy and freedom in Europe when these values were clearly lacking in the United States. President Wilson said, "The world must be made safe for democracy."[6] But many blacks wondered what he was doing to make the United States safe for democracy.

Other blacks, however, hoped the war would be a tool they could use in the fight for racial equality. They hoped military service would lead, as black leader W. E. B. Du Bois had said, to "the right to vote and the right to work and the right to live without insult."[7] Most African Americans supported the war effort. They saw the war as a chance to prove their loyalty to their country. If they answered the call to arms, surely their country would be forced to acknowledge them as full citizens deserving equal treatment and consideration under the law. Du Bois urged African Americans to enlist: "Let us, while this war lasts, forget our special grievances and close ranks shoulder to shoulder with our

RESISTING THE CALL TO ARMS

Not all African Americans supported the war. African-American leader A. Chandler Owen spoke out against African Americans joining the war effort. He pointed out that military service in the past hadn't done much to improve the condition of blacks in the United States: "Did not the Negro fight in the Revolutionary War, with Crispus Attucks dying first . . . and come out to be a miserable chattel slave in this country for nearly one hundred years?"[8]

own white fellow citizens and the allied nations that are fighting for democracy. We make no ordinary sacrifice, but we make it gladly and willingly."[9]

By June 15, 1917, Hayward had 2,002 men recruited—two more than necessary for the first National Guard unit in New York to reach combat strength.[10] Usually, National Guard units did not fight overseas, but the US declaration of war meant a national emergency, and men were needed for the fight in Europe. By July, Hayward had 2,053 and an additional 54 officers.[11] The next step was to get the men into the fight. Hayward wanted his men to be the first New York unit to fight in France.

W. E. B. DU BOIS

Born shortly after the Civil War, on February 23, 1868, W. E. B. Du Bois was one of the most important African Americans in US history. A prominent black leader and intellectual, Du Bois was the first African American to earn a PhD from Harvard (1895). He published more than 300 speeches, 23 books, and 400 articles, to name just some of his work. He helped found the National Association for the Advancement of Colored People (NAACP) and served as editor of its magazine, the *Crisis*. Du Bois urged African Americans to support the US war effort. He opposed military segregation but worked to help establish an officers training camp for African Americans, hoping black troops could have black officers. After World War I, Du Bois organized an international meeting. The Pan-African Congress of 1919 sought to end colonial rule and racial discrimination.

If African Americans were not banned from a certain branch of the military, they were forced to serve as messmen or laborers instead of fighting in combat.

CHAPTER
★ 5 ★

WAR IN EUROPE AND WAR AT HOME

The Fifteenth National Guard unit was formed largely due to the US military's policy of segregating black and white troops. Not only did the military segregate troops, but it also excluded blacks from certain assignments in the military. For example, African Americans were banned from serving in the US Marines. In the navy, African Americans were allowed to work only as messmen (the navy equivalent of waiters), and in the US Army Air Corps, blacks couldn't train as pilots; they could only serve as ground crew. Most black army troops were assigned to labor companies as part of the Service of Supply (SOS), or as stevedores who loaded freight onto or off of ships. Only a few were allowed in combat, and most of these were in the infantry rather than artillery units.

DISCRIMINATION IN THE MILITARY

Discrimination was even more apparent when it came to officers. Approximately 400,000 black soldiers served in World War I, yet only 1,200 of these soldiers served under a black officer.[1] Some African-American leaders, including Du Bois, felt that if there was going to be segregation in the military, then black units should at least have black officers. Fort Des Moines, an all-black officer training camp, finally opened in 1917 in Des Moines, Iowa, with 1,250 men enrolled.[2]

Plenty of whites, especially southern whites, didn't want black officers or black troops at all. Given the lawless injustice and abuse blacks regularly faced, southern whites in particular did not want black men armed with guns. They also didn't want blacks shooting whites, even if they were enemy German troops.

OFFICER TRAINING CAMP AT FORT DES MOINES

In June 1917, the black officer training camp opened at Fort Des Moines, Iowa. The first class of 639 officers graduated on October 17, 1917. By the time the camp closed at the end of the war, there were 1,400 black commissioned officers, yet white officers continued to command black units.[3]

Some black leaders opposed the camp at Fort Des Moines, saying it was just another version of Jim Crow.

RACIAL PROBLEMS OF 1917

Racial tension was on the rise, and the summer of 1917 was a particularly explosive time. On July 1, 1917, one of the worst race riots in US history broke out in East Saint Louis, Illinois.

Then, on August 23, at Camp Logan, near Houston, Texas, a group of African-American soldiers reacted to racial discrimination and segregation. Most military training facilities were in the South, and southern towns were segregated and typically hostile toward black troops, particularly northern black troops. African-American troops heard rumors that a black soldier had been shot and an armed mob was heading toward camp. Angered by the East Saint Louis riots and fed up with segregation and racial insults, black troops from the Twenty-Fourth Infantry seized weapons and marched into Houston, killing 19 people, including four black soldiers and four police officers.

During this tense time, the Fifteenth New York National Guard Regiment got orders to leave for training at Camp Whitman, near Poughkeepsie, New York, on July 15, 1917. After two weeks of basic training in tasks such as drills, saluting, and removing lice from clothing, the men went on active duty. Some soldiers guarded New York railroad lines; others did construction or guarded suspected German spies at Ellis Island.

NO PARADE FOR THE FIFTEENTH

When Hayward learned about a farewell parade being planned on August 30, 1917, for troops from the Twenty-Seventh Division heading to final training before deployment to France, he begged to be included in the parade.

RIOTING IN EAST SAINT LOUIS

The race riots in East Saint Louis, Illinois, began on May 28, 1917, when white union workers went on strike at a local factory. The factory then called in black strikebreakers to work. Many of these blacks had recently migrated to East Saint Louis from the South. These black workers replaced the white workers who were on strike. Angry at the black workers who had taken their jobs, a white mob of more than 3,000 destroyed African-American stores, homes, and churches. On July 2, eyewitnesses reported that African Americans were shot as they ran from their burning homes. More than 100 African Americans lost their lives in the riot.[4]

Militia stands by and watches as a mob beats an African-American man in front of a street car during the East Saint Louis riots.

The Twenty-Seventh "Rainbow" division was made up of guard units from 27 different states, and Hayward wanted his men to march. Instead, he was told black was not a color of the rainbow. Back at headquarters, Colonel Hayward raised his right hand and swore an oath to his men: "Even if they won't let us parade with them in going away . . . we will have a parade when we come home that will be the greatest parade . . . that New York has ever seen." Then he made his men stand and swear with him, "that whichever [of us] may be in survival as commanding officer of this regiment when we get back to New York, that we see to it that the glory and the honor of the Negro race in America may be served by having our welcome home parade celebrated." All the men joined hands and said, "Amen!"[5]

A WARNING

After the Houston riots, the commanding officer of the black training camp in Fort Des Moines, Major General Charles C. Ballou, issued a bulletin to black men serving in the Ninety-Second Division. He warned African-American troops of the consequences of not obeying local segregation laws: "White men made the Division, and they can break it just as easily if it becomes a trouble maker."[6]

Colonel Hayward was white and his troops were black, but he was proud of his men and fiercely loyal to them. He respected his men, and they in turn respected him. He worked diligently to get fair treatment for his men and give them the same opportunities white troops had. And one opportunity black troops didn't have was the right to fight.

When Hayward got word his men were being sent to Spartanburg, South Carolina, for training, he knew the situation would be explosive given the racist attitudes of most southerners. The War Department knew that as well. But to be fair, the US military was sending northern troops south and southern troops north, and as far as the War Department was concerned, its job was to fight the war in Europe, not the racial conflicts in the states. As Secretary of War Newton Baker said, "There is no intention on the part of the War Department to undertake at this time to settle the so-called race question."[7] In fact, it seemed as if it wanted to simply ignore the current racial unrest. However, given the racial mood in the country, sending 2,000 black troops, especially northern black troops, to train in South Carolina was asking for trouble.

One of Hayward's white officers, Hamilton Fish, tried to use his influence to head off disaster. Fish wrote to a family friend, future president Franklin Delano Roosevelt (then working as the assistant secretary of the navy in Washington, DC) and suggested the War Department send the Fifteenth straight to France and avoid Spartanburg altogether: "This battalion could render immediate valuable service in France. . . . Why not solve difficult southern problem by letting these northern Negro soldiers go where they can be of immediate use and train for firing line quicker than in the south?"[8]

EXPLOSIVE SPARTANBURG

Nevertheless, on October 8, 1917, the Fighting Fifteenth found themselves on their way to Spartanburg for training, along with other New York National Guard units. And sure enough, they had problems with southern whites starting the very first night. A group of four black and four white soldiers were walking together down the sidewalk when some young white men started yelling racial insults. Although the black soldiers stayed out of it, the white soldiers started throwing punches at the troublemakers. Throughout the regiment's uneasy stay in Spartanburg, white northern troops stood by the Fifteenth.

The very next day, Colonel Hayward gathered his men together, climbed on the roof of a shed so they could all see and hear him, and urged them not to respond to the ignorance of the local citizens. Hayward asked for restraint:

> *You are camped in a region hostile to colored people. I am depending on you to act like the good soldiers you have always been and break the ice in this country for your entire race. We are about to win the regiment's greatest victory.*[9]

He then asked all his men to raise their right hands and swear to refrain from violence. The men raised their hands and pledged.

Hayward and Fish met with local officials and businessmen, urging calm. The regimental band played local concerts as a way to build goodwill. Fish also met with the local mayor and town council and told them if any local whites caused problems for the Fifteenth, Fish would take legal action.

But problems kept cropping up, and everyone was on edge. For instance, black officer Captain Napoleon Bonaparte Marshall bought a ticket to ride the trolley. Once aboard, he was called racial slurs and thrown off. Another time, black soldiers heard a rumor that two black soldiers had been lynched. Forty armed soldiers went to the police station to check. Hayward raced to the station as well and helped prevent a riot.

Racial tensions were sure to get worse. If the Fifteenth stayed, there would be serious trouble. But if they moved to a different training camp, southern whites would think harassment was a good strategy. The third option was to ship the Fifteenth to France. On October 18, 1917, Hayward went to Washington, DC, for a secret meeting with the secretary of war to urge that his men be shipped to France immediately. Hayward knew he had to get his men out of Spartanburg, and fast.

Hamilton Fish, *right*, shown here with General Mark L. Hersey, *left*, hoped to avoid violence in Spartanburg.

OFF TO FRANCE

Hayward's plea was answered. He returned to Spartanburg and announced to his white officers that the Fifteenth would be leaving for France in a few days. Meanwhile, African-American Emmett Scott, special assistant to the secretary of war, met privately with black officers of the Fifteenth. In an emotional meeting, these men expressed their bitterness at the mistreatment and injustice they had endured, but they agreed they would not retaliate.

On October 24, 1917, only two weeks after arriving in Spartanburg, the Fifteenth left for France. As they marched in formation to the train station, thousands of white troops, the Seventh

Troops training at Camp Wadsworth in Spartanburg, South Carolina

and Twelfth Regiments from New York, lined the road to honor them. As the Fighting Fifteenth marched by, men from the Twenty-Seventh began singing the famous World War I war tune "Over There." The Fifteenth was on its way to France at last.

EMMETT SCOTT

From 1897 to 1915, Emmett Scott worked as the private secretary and personal assistant to African-American leader and educator Booker T. Washington. After Washington's death in 1915, Scott moved to Washington, DC, in 1917 to serve as special assistant to Secretary of War Newton Baker. After the war, Scott wrote a detailed history called *The American Negro in the First World War.*

The Fifteenth New York National Guard Regiment arrived in Brest, France, in December 1917, on board the USS *Pocahontas*.

THE FIGHTING FIFTEENTH IN FRANCE

After leaving Spartanburg on October 24, 1917, the Fifteenth
New York National Guard Regiment went to Camp Mills in Long
Island, New York. Fearing German spies, the War Department kept
the regiment's departure a secret. On November 12, 1917, the
Fifteenth New York National Guard boarded the transport ship
USS *Pocahontas*, but it took them four tries to actually leave. First
the ship developed a mechanical problem 200 miles (320 km) out
to sea and had to return to port. Then the ship's coal caught fire
after their second departure on December 3. They left again on
December 12, but blizzard conditions led to a collision with
a tanker in New York Harbor. Finally, they made it safely out of

After arriving in France and completing their brief training, the Fifteenth was still assigned to work crews.

New York Harbor, avoided German submarines, and landed at the harbor in Brest, France, on December 27, 1917. When the Fifteenth arrived in France, they had had only three weeks of training.

SAINT-NAZAIRE, FRANCE

Sure enough, when the Fifteenth arrived, they were put to work. Instead of heading east to the front, the Fifteenth was sent to the port city of

Saint-Nazaire, France, nicknamed "Stench Nazaire" by US troops. General John J. Pershing, commander of all US forces, wanted Saint-Nazaire readied as a key port for US troops. Although the work in Saint-Nazaire was critical to the war effort, the men of the Fifteenth, including Colonel Hayward, were frustrated by their assignment to work crews. According to Colonel Hayward, "Here the regiment toiled for weeks building docks, erecting hospitals, laying railroad tracks and constructing a great dam. The men never saw their rifles except by candle light."[1]

THE REGIMENTAL BAND GOES ON TOUR

Meanwhile, the regimental band was sent on a goodwill tour that would help spread the fame of the Fighting Fifteenth far and wide. On February 12, 1918, Lieutenant James Reese Europe and his regimental band boarded a train for a concert tour of 25 French cities. The treatment they received was a far cry from the segregation and racial discrimination of the United States. Europe rode in a first-class coach

ENTERTAINING THE TROOPS

While the Fifteenth was stationed at Saint-Nazaire, New York theatrical producer Winthrop Ames was in France organizing shows to entertain US troops. He heard about the talented Fifteenth regimental band, but he was doubtful. He'd heard plenty of military bands already, and they were average at best. Colonel Hayward invited Ames to a concert, and Ames couldn't believe what he heard: "No sooner had they began to play than it became obvious that we were not listening to the ordinary army band at all, but to an organization of the very highest quality, trained and led by a conductor of genius."[2]

JAMES REESE EUROPE

1881–1919

James Reese Europe was born in Mobile, Alabama, in 1881. He studied violin, piano, and composition, and after his father died in 1900, he moved to New York City to pursue a musical career. Although he dreamed of a National Negro Symphony Orchestra, Europe got work composing and playing popular music. One of Europe's biggest talents was organizing musicians and lining up gigs, or paid musical performances. In 1910, Europe organized the Clef Club of New York, a black musician's union. Under Europe's leadership, Clef Club musicians played for the lavish private parties of wealthy New Yorkers. In 1913, Europe's orchestra became the first black orchestra offered a record contract.

Hayward asked Europe to organize a regimental band in 1916. Europe made the Fifteenth regimental band famous throughout France as he introduced Europeans to ragtime and jazz. Europe was also the first black American officer to lead troops in World War I combat. After returning to the United States, he organized a nationwide tour for the regimental band. A few months into the tour, however, Europe's career was cut short when irate band member Herbert Wright stabbed him backstage. Europe died on May 9, 1919. After a public funeral, Europe was buried in Arlington National Cemetery. With more than 100 musical works to his credit, Europe opened new doors for black musicians and for African-American music.

car, which he shared with one other person: the white Major Arthur Little. The rest of the band rode in second-class cars.

As the train chugged toward its final destination, the resort town of Aix-les-Bains, it stopped at towns along the way so the band could play short concerts in town squares. On February 15, the train pulled into Aix-les-Bains, a town chosen as an official spot for rest and recuperation for US military officers and troops. The band was so popular their original 16-day tour was extended two more weeks. They played three concerts a day filled with everything from ragtime and vaudeville to classical music, in addition to hymns for religious services and concerts in the park.

PUSHING FOR COMBAT

While the band kept at its hectic concert schedule, Colonel Hayward kept pressing General Pershing for a combat assignment. Hayward was determined his men deserved the right to fight. The British and French kept pressing Pershing for troops as well. Pershing wanted US troops to fight under US commanders, and US policy under President Wilson opposed putting blacks in combat. But on March 10, 1918, Pershing finally agreed to send four black infantry regiments to the French front lines, including the Fifteenth New York National Guard Regiment.

Pershing's decision was undoubtedly influenced by a treaty signed a week earlier, on March 3, 1918, that ended fighting between Russia and Germany. In 1917, there had been a revolution in Russia, and the new Russian government wanted out of the war. With Russia out of the war, Germany no longer had to fight on two fronts, and it was pushing to win the war before US troops arrived in full force. France desperately needed additional troops, such as the Fifteenth, to help fend off the additional German forces heading toward France.

BRINGING RACISM TO FRANCE

Despite the band's popularity, black troops could not visit rest areas such as Aix-les-Bains because, following US procedure, the rest areas were "whites only." The band could come and play, but neither the band nor any black soldiers could come to Aix-les-Bains on leave. Hayward protested this unfair treatment, but nothing changed. Although white French troops accepted black soldiers as equals, many white US troops did not. Racist US attitudes followed black troops to France. In August 1918, US officers pressured the French to send a secret memo, called "Secret Information concerning Black American Troops," to French officers. The report warned the French not to treat blacks as equals. It stated the French should "prevent the rise of any pronounced degree of intimacy. . . . [W]e cannot deal with them on the same plane as white American officers." They also should not "commend too highly the black American troops, particularly in the presence of (white) Americans." The French were told to not "spoil" the black soldiers and to keep them away from white French women. The document said that "although a citizen of the United States, the black man is regarded by the white American as an inferior being."[3] The French paid little attention to this memo and continued to treat black troops as they always had.

JOINING THE FOURTH FRENCH ARMY

Now that the Fifteenth was being sent into combat, they were renamed the 369th Infantry Regiment of the US Army and assigned to serve under the Sixteenth Division of the Fourth French Army. In some ways, the assignment was an insult. The first insult was their assigned number—369. Numbers higher than 200 were assigned to troops who had been drafted, or forced to sign up. But the men of the Fifteenth weren't draftees—they had volunteered to serve. Second, Pershing had given Hayward's regiment to the French rather than include them in the American Expeditionary Force. As Hayward put it, "Our great American general simply put the black orphan in a basket, set it on the doorstep of the French, pulled the bell, and went away."[4]

All the same, a combat unit—any combat unit—was better than a labor unit. In a letter to another commanding officer, Hayward wrote, "The most wonderful thing in the world has happened to this regiment. A fairy tale has materialized and a beautiful dream has come true. We are now a combat unit . . . assigned to a sector of trenches."[5] For the rest of the war, the Fifteenth, now renamed the 369th, would serve as part of the French army.

TRAINING WITH THE FRENCH

By March 21, 1918, the band and the regiment had reunited at the town of Herpont, France, to begin training under the French command. The most notable

The regimental band plays in France.

difference about the French was their relative lack of racism compared with Americans. Colonel Hayward wrote to Emmett Scott, "The French soldiers have not the slightest prejudice or feeling. The [French soldiers] and my boys are great chums, eat, dance, sing, march and fight together in absolute accord."[6]

Noble Sissle, band major and great friend of James Europe, wrote of the comradeship:

> *The French officers had taken our officers and made pals of them. . . . Cheeriest of all was the good comradeship that existed between our enlisted men and the faithful old French poilu [soldier]. You could see them strolling down the road, arm in arm, each hardly able to understand the other, as our boys' French was as bad as their English.*[7]

The French were used to black troops. Black African soldiers from the French colonies had been fighting in Europe since 1914.

The US 369th traded in their US uniforms for French ones, which included blue-gray French helmets and French Lebel rifles with bayonets, which were noticeably worse than the American Springfield rifles. Their equipment, supplies, and food, which was noticeably better than US food, also came from the French. After roughly three weeks of training in the French reserve lines, the men of the 369th were ready to move to the front lines and into the largest series of battles in the history of the world at that time: the 1918 German spring offensive.

BRINGING JAZZ TO FRANCE

While in France, James Reese Europe and his band introduced and popularized the new sounds of ragtime and jazz. Ragtime music first appeared in the 1890s, closely followed by jazz in the 1910s. These types of music have African-American roots. When African slaves were first brought to America in the 1700s, they developed their own distinctive music. Ragtime music developed from African-American dance styles. As blues, ragtime, and dance music mixed, jazz was born. Noble Sissle, drum major and vocalist for the band, joked that the "Jazz germ" had come to France: "Colonel Hayward has brought his band over here and started ragtimitis in France; ain't this an awful thing to visit upon a nation with so many burdens?"[8]

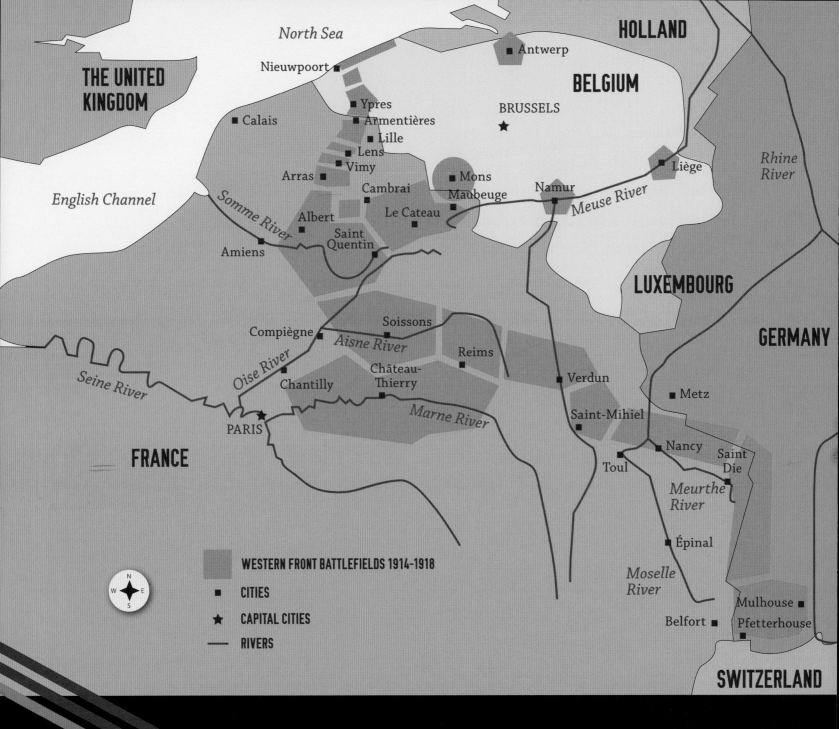

The western front

AT THE FRONT

After signing a separate peace treaty with the Russians on March 3, 1918, the Germans turned their full force to the western front. For their 1918 spring offensive, Germany transferred an additional 20 divisions to the western front, with each division composed of 10,000 to 18,000 fighters.[1] On March 21, 1918, the Germans launched a massive attack, hoping to conquer France before any more US troops could arrive. The Germans were at first successful. They pushed harder and captured 40 miles (64 km) out of 50 miles (80 km) of British-held territory. By the beginning of May, the Germans were 40 miles (64 km) from Paris, France.

Heading into this massive offensive, the 369th moved to the front on April 13, 1918. Troops were rotated ten days in the support line, ten days in the front line, and ten days in the reserve

Although it was mostly on the defense, the 369th fought impressively.

line. Their task was to defend the right flank against German attack, a 2.8-mile (4.5 km) stretch of territory, which at the time was 20 percent of the territory US troops held. During the first weeks at the front, the 369th was mostly on the defensive, facing daily artillery fire and raids from German parties. Their heroism was impressive. For example, Johnson and Roberts withstood an attack by more than 24 German troops on May 15, 1918.

UNDER FIRE

During World War I, only 10 percent of black troops were assigned to combat units.[2] Some in the War Department doubted black soldiers could perform well under the new warfare of World War I. World War I had changed how wars were fought. Warfare no longer consisted of men charging on horseback with swords or infantry soldiers marching in formation. War was now mechanized with machine guns, artillery fire, poison gas, and tanks. But the Hellfighters bore trench warfare just as any other troops, sometimes better. Unlike African troops or whites from rural areas, the Harlem troops were unfazed by the sudden, deafening noises ever-present on the frontline trenches. At one point, 16 Hellfighters withstood more than five straight hours of artillery fire in order to send signal flares that would reveal the enemy's location.[3]

DAILY LIFE IN THE TRENCHES

Daily life in the trenches could be surprisingly routine. If no attack came at dawn, men then ate breakfast and started on various chores, such as cleaning weapons, repairing trenches, and checking their feet for the disease called trench foot. Trench foot was caused by the damp, cold, and dirty conditions of the trenches. Trench foot led feet to became numb and discolored with a foul odor. As the condition worsened, feet would swell and become infected. If left untreated, trench foot could lead to gangrene and the need to amputate the infected foot.

When not fighting, men might nap or write letters. Darkness brought more dangerous assignments, such as manning observation posts, repairing barbed wire defenses, digging trenches a little closer to the enemy, or, most dangerous of all, attacking the enemy in a raiding party.

In late spring, the US Army began sending more black troops to the 369th. These new soldiers concerned Colonel Hayward because they were untrained draftees, usually from the rural south, and they were often illiterate and uneducated. They also lacked a strong sense of loyalty to the Fifteenth National Guard Regiment and all it stood for. Both Hayward and the French commanders protested that these new, untrained troops were not ready to fight, often refused to fight, and dragged down the confidence, enthusiasm, and discipline of the unit. Nevertheless, the 369th swelled from 2,000 to 3,000 until 5,000 men had served in the regiment.[4]

THE CHAMPAGNE-MARNE DEFENSIVE

In early July, Colonel Hayward received word from French general Henri Gouraud the Germans were preparing for a large-scale attack. Gouraud hoped to lure the Germans into a trap by evacuating the forward trenches, leaving just a few men as

MUSIC IN THE TRENCHES

James Reese Europe not only led the regimental band but also fought in the trenches and served as lieutenant in a machine-gun company. When he and drum major Noble Sissle rotated to the rear, they borrowed a piano from a local French family. They moved the piano to their barracks, or living quarters, so they could play and sing. Europe also borrowed a small pump organ from a chaplain and brought it to the support trenches so he could play tunes in the dugouts to entertain the troops. He wrote songs throughout World War I. These wartime songs had titles such as "Trench Trot," "I've Got the Map of Your Heart," and "On Patrol in No Man's Land."

decoys. Then, when the Germans moved into the abandoned trenches, the French would open fire.

On July 14, Bastille Day (France's Independence Day), the Germans attacked. Private Herbert White wrote, "About midnight the Germans threw one of the heaviest bombardments of their four years of warfare. . . . For miles and miles all you could see was the flash of the big guns and the continuous roar of cannon and bursting of shells."[5] The shelling was nearly constant. But by July 15, the Allies had broken the German forces and begun to counterattack. At one point during this battle, the 369th was fighting near the Sixty-Ninth Infantry, the so-called Rainbow Division that had refused to parade with the Hellfighters. To its dismay, the Rainbow Division lost ground as the Germans broke through their line. The Hellfighters, on the other hand, held their ground.

GENERAL HENRI GOURAUD

The 369th served as part of the French Fourth Army, which General Henri Gouraud commanded. Known as the Lion of France, General Gouraud was France's youngest general, but one of its most experienced. He lost his right arm early in the war and limped from a leg injury, but Gouraud recovered and took command of the French Fourth Army in July 1917. The troops respected and admired Gouraud. During a concert, Gouraud asked Noble Sissle to sing the French song "Joan of Arc." According to Sissle,

Though [the general's] eyes seemed to be dimmed with tears, yet there flashed a light from them that literally burned with all the fire and courage for which this great warrior was known . . . to challenge the hostile foe that France might live and enjoy her freedom.[6]

During the battle on July 15, German troops never broke through the Hellfighters' line.

THE TIDE TURNS

July 15 through July 17, 1918, marked the turning point of the war as the Germans began to retreat. But the war was far from over. Another major battle, the Meuse-Argonne Offensive, began on September 26, 1918. On the first day of this battle, the 369th captured a town that had been held by Germans. This day marked the heaviest fighting the 369th endured during the entire war. In one day, they were reduced from 20 officers to seven and from 700 men to only 150.[7]

The next day, they pushed forward only 0.6 miles (1 km). On September 30, they captured an important railroad junction. In just a few days, the 369th had 851 casualties: 172 dead and 679 wounded.[8]

On the night of September 30, 1918, the 369th was finally relieved by the French 363rd Infantry, and the Hellfighters remained in reserve until October 7. During October, as the German army retreated, the 369th, as part of the French army, pushed into the territory that had been occupied by the Germans.

HARLEM HELLFIGHTER HEROES

The 369th regiment was one of the most relentless, thanks to its many war heroes. One of these heroes was Horace Pippin, who in July 1918 volunteered to hunt down a sniper who had been shooting Hellfighters from a hidden position. Pippin and another volunteer searched all night in the rain, but they couldn't find the sniper. Daylight arrived, and Pippin kept looking. He spotted a tree where the sniper might be hiding, so Pippin stayed out of sight and waited for shots to reveal the sniper's position. Pippin was wet and cold. He'd been up all night in the rain, and as noon approached, he considered giving up. But then he saw the leaves of the tree move. He aimed his rifle and fired. If he missed, he would reveal his position. But Pippin's aim was true, and the dead sniper fell to the ground.

Another one of these men was Captain Charles Fillmore, who saw his men start to panic as they moved through a low-lying swamp containing poisonous gas on July 21, 1918. Fillmore knew it was not deadly gas; instead, it was gas that irritated, causing headaches and nausea. But his men were terrified, and their urge was to run, not calmly move to higher ground. To show his men they would make it through, Fillmore deliberately removed his gas mask and endured a gassing. He then calmly led his men to safety on higher ground.

Finally, the fighting ceased. At 11 a.m. on the eleventh day of the eleventh month, 1918, World War I ended, and Germany signed an armistice agreement with the Allied powers. Allied troops prepared to move in to temporarily occupy Germany, and the Harlem Hellfighters were the first Allied unit to reach the Rhine River, the border between France and Germany, on November 17, 1918.

COURAGE OF THE 369TH

The 369th regiment had endured much since they left New York in December 1917. In their 191 days of combat—more than any other US regiment—the 369th never lost a foot of ground, and they never had a man taken prisoner. The regiment known first as the Fifteenth New York National Guard, then the 369th

Infantry Regiment of the US Army, was now known as the Harlem Hellfighters. Of the almost 2,100 original men, roughly 1,500 had been killed or wounded.[9] These African-American men had fought bravely.

The French acknowledged the extraordinary valor of the 369th by awarding 171 Croix de Guerre.[10] Honors from the US government were deserved but few were given out. Colonel Hayward, however, kept his promise. He made sure his Hellfighters got their own parade down the streets of New York.

THE FRENCH CROIX DE GUERRE

In 1915, the French government established the military honor the Croix de Guerre (War Cross). The Croix de Guerre honored acts of bravery in the face of the enemy. The Croix de Guerre medal was a Maltese cross placed over crossed swords. In the center of the cross is a helmeted profile of a female, which symbolizes the French Republic. The Croix de Guerre was awarded to both military units and individuals. The 369th received a unit Croix de Guerre as well as earning 170 individual citations for the soldiers, a total of 171.

Harlem Hellfighters wave as they approach home on February 12, 1919.

THE BOYS COME HOME

The Harlem Hellfighters were exceptional, both as fighters and as representatives of the United States during World War I. Besides serving 191 days on the front line, the Hellfighters were part of many firsts during World War I. They were the first National Guard unit in New York to reach combat strength, the first African-American troops in World War I combat, and the first Allied troops to reach the Rhine River on November 17, 1918. Two members, Johnson and Roberts, were the first Americans to receive the Croix de Guerre, and Lieutenant James Reese Europe was the first black officer to lead troops in World War I combat. And after the war, the Harlem Hellfighters would also be the first US combat troops to come home.

On December 17, 1918, the French command officially released the 369th from service. In January 1919, as diplomats prepared for peace talks in Paris, the Harlem Hellfighters prepared to return home. They made their way back to Brest, the same port town they had departed six months earlier, and sailed for New York on January 31. The journey took almost two weeks. On February 12, they reached the New York Harbor where the Statue of Liberty stood.

LOOKING LIKE A SOLDIER

For their victory parade, the men of the Fifteenth looked every bit the soldier. The *World* newspaper reported: "At an exact angle over their right shoulders were their long-bayonetted rifles. Around their waists were belts of cartridges [bullets]. On their heads were their 'tin hats,' the steel helmets that saved many a life, as was attested by the dents and scars in some of them. Their eyes were straight forward and their chins, held high naturally, seemed higher than ever because of the leather straps that circled them. The fighters wore spiral puttees [leg coverings like stockings] and their heavy hobbed hiking shoes, which caused a metallic clash as they scraped over the asphalt."[3]

VICTORY PARADE

When Colonel Hayward first organized the Fifteenth New York National Guard Regiment in June 1916, the men had marched in vacant lots with brooms instead of guns. On February 17, 1919, the 369th was given a victory parade the likes of which New York had never seen. One newspaper estimated a crowd of more than 250,000 people.[1] Another paper estimated approximately 2 million. Still another said 5 million.[2] According to the *New York*

Family members and citizens packed the streets of New York to see the victory parade.

Times, "The sidewalks were packed [for blocks] like a subway train at the rush hour."[4]

Beginning at Madison Square Park, the 369th marched up Fifth Avenue heading toward Harlem. They marched in tight formation, French style, stepping in time to the music of James Reese Europe and his regimental band. At the head

The Harlem Hellfighters march along Fifth Avenue.

of the parade rode four platoons of mounted police; then walking alone on foot was Colonel Hayward. A leg injury during the war had left him with a limp, but he marched on foot at the head of the regiment. Colonel Hayward's staff marched behind him, then a police band, and then the band everyone really wanted to hear: Europe's regimental band. The regimental band played many of the military marches that were French favorites, such as "The Salute to the 85th."

Behind the regimental band came the rows of soldiers in full uniform with bayonetted rifles perfectly angled against their right shoulders. Throughout the war, the 369th had carried the state flag of New York with them. They now marched proudly up Fifth Avenue carrying it still, as New Yorkers cheered. Next in the parade came automobiles and ambulances carrying injured and wounded officers and soldiers.

THE PRAISE OF HARLEM

"The real height of the enthusiasm was reached when . . . the heroes arrived in the real Black Belt of Harlem. This was the Home, Sweet Home for hundreds of them, the neighborhood they'd been born in and had grown up in, and from 129 Street north the windows and roofs and fire escapes of the five and six story apartment houses were filled to overflowing with their nearest and dearest."[5] —*World* newspaper, February 18, 1919

Riding in an open car was the now-famous Private Henry Johnson, the first American to receive the Croix de Guerre. Johnson stood in the car as it rolled along, bowing and waving to the crowd.

Private Johnson waves to the crowd.

On the Hellfighters marched as the crowd cheered and waved flags. The parade paused briefly in front of the reviewing stand, which was a platform full of important politicians and dignitaries including New York governor Al Smith and former New York governor Whitman, who had authorized the all-black regiment.

The regimental band played military marches until they got to Harlem. Then they swung into the ragtime tune "Here Comes My Daddy Now!" It was a catchy tune with a chorus that began, "Here comes my daaaaa-ddy now. Oh pop! Oh pop! Oh pop!" The band played ragtime and jazz as they marched down the Harlem streets, the crowd cheering so loudly at times people couldn't even hear the band. After the parade, the 369th celebrated with a dinner held in their honor. It was a well-deserved and glorious day, far beyond even Colonel Hayward's expectations.

DIGNITARIES AT THE PARADE

Several important officials and well-known New Yorkers were on the reviewing stand:

- Governor Al Smith
- Former governor Charles Whitman
- Emmett Scott, assistant to Secretary of War Newton Baker
- Mrs. Vincent Astor, wife of a millionaire businessman
- Rodman Wanamaker, influential businessman and founder of a department store chain
- William Randolph Hearst, founder of a newspaper empire

The Harlem Hellfighters helped shape a better opinion of African-American soldiers, but the issue of race was far from resolved.

AFTERMATH OF BIRACIAL WARFARE

On February 18, 1919, the men of the 369th were released from active military service. They were lucky to have survived. During the four years of the war, an estimated 20 million people died, half of whom were from the general population.[1] Global empires were destroyed and new governments came to power.

World War I devastated the United States less than other countries. The United States was involved for only 19 months, and the US economy and military were actually stronger at the end of the war than at the beginning. For African Americans, the war's impact was greater. World War I included African-American soldiers in record numbers. Before the war, some Americans viewed black soldiers as almost comic, not worth taking seriously. The Hellfighters and other black troops changed that view.

In France, African Americans had experienced a level of equality and acceptance greater than any they had ever known. Blacks and whites mingled together in society. Men and women of different races socialized openly together. There was no segregation, except in areas governed by the US military. Blacks in France were often not assumed to be inferior. As one officer said, "The French people knew no color line."[2]

FIGHTING BACK

African Americans expected returning black soldiers to receive a hero's welcome similar to the Hellfighters' parade and to be treated with a new respect and equality. But racism and violence continued. African Americans' experiences in France made blacks, particularly black soldiers, feel even more keenly the injustices of their own country, a country they had fought and died for. They hoped their patriotic sacrifices would create positive change, but conditions hadn't seemed to change at all, or perhaps were even getting worse.

The number of lynchings rose during the war. Some of these lynching victims were African-American soldiers home from the war, still in uniform. The Ku Klux Klan (KKK)—a secret organization that believed in white superiority and was opposed to blacks, Catholics, and Jews—spread into northern states. The

Ku Klux Klan members dressed all in white.

summer of 1919 was called the Red Summer because there were so many bloody clashes between whites and blacks. There were 25 race riots, similar to the 1917 one in East Saint Louis, during the Red Summer. The worst of these was the Chicago Riot of 1919, which began on July 27 when an African-American teenager swimming in Lake Michigan drifted into an area reserved for whites. He was stoned and drowned. When police refused to arrest the white men involved, fighting broke out.

Against this backdrop of racism, some blacks felt their service in the war changed nothing. As Emmett Scott told a group of black veterans, "As anyone who recalls the assurances of 1917 and 1918, I confess personally a deep sense of disappointment of poignant pain, that a great country in time of need should promise so much and afterward perform so little."[3]

RACIAL PRIDE

But things had changed. The war and the racial pride it created led to a new fighting spirit for equality. Black soldiers had been good citizens, and now they were going to hold their country accountable. African Americans were tired of asking for equality. They were ready to demand it. This spirit of determination surged throughout black communities as racially militant newspapers, magazines, and political organizations developed. The black press gave veterans an outlet to express their anger and frustration. Du Bois wrote:

White spectators look on the murdered, mutilated, and burned body of Will Brown during the Red Summer of 1919.

We return.

We return from fighting.

We return fighting.

Make way for Democracy! We saved it in France, and by the great Jehovah, we will save it in the United States of America, or know the reason why.[4]

PEACE TALKS IN PARIS

Preliminary peace talks began in Paris on January 4, 1919. These talks led to a series of treaties between the Allies and the Central powers. The Treaty of Versailles between the Allies and Germany was signed on June 28, 1919, exactly five years after the assassination of Archduke Ferdinand, the event that sparked the war. The Treaty of Saint-Germain with Austria was signed on September 10, 1919, and the Treaty of Trianon with Hungary was signed on June 4, 1920. The United States did not sign a peace treaty with Germany until August 25, 1921.

In addition to this new militant spirit, the war contributed to a new sense of internationalism. Due to the war, Du Bois and other African Americans felt more a part of international movements across the globe. In 1919, Du Bois organized a Pan-African Congress, held in Paris during the World War I peace talks. His goal was to challenge European colonialism and promote freedom for colonized nations. The Russian Revolution and the political theories of communism also contributed to this new internationalism and influenced some black writers and artists.

African-American artists and musicians, such as Louis Armstrong, rose to fame during the Harlem Renaissance.

The sense of black pride and action made fertile ground for the flowering of African-American culture and literature known as the Harlem Renaissance. The Harlem Renaissance occurred from the end of World War I until the mid-1930s.

It was a period when cultural, artistic, and social ideas thrived. James Europe contributed to the rise of the Harlem Renaissance when he spread the seeds of jazz throughout France.

Serving in France had provided new opportunities for all African-American troops, not just the Harlem Hellfighters. Particularly for blacks from the rural south, military service provided black soldiers with benefits they had never known before, such as basic health care, the opportunity to learn to read and write, and contact with a wider range of people.

CREATING A MORE EQUAL MILITARY

After the war, the military shrank, particularly the number of African Americans serving. Only 1.5 percent of the military was African-American by the summer of 1940.[5] Although the military generally kept African Americans in service roles rather than combat, black units continued to push for the right to fight. In early 1941, the US Army announced its first African-American Air Corps unit, the famed Tuskegee Airmen. The number of black soldiers in combat and leadership positions slowly grew,

NEW NEGRO MOVEMENT

After World War I, scholar Alain Locke said returning veterans had sparked a new mood among African Americans. In *The New Negro,* he said a "new negro" had arisen, one that had a different spirit than that of former black leaders such as Booker T. Washington.[6] The "old negro" would settle for whatever white men would stoop to give. The "new negro" would settle for nothing less than full equality and participation.

but official segregation in the military continued until 1948.

After World War I, the 369th never saw combat again. But in the mid-1930s, it became the first National Guard unit with all-black officers, as Colonel Hayward had hoped. One of its commanders, Colonel Benjamin O. Davis Sr., became the first African-American general in the US Army. The battle for racial equality and equal justice under the law was far from over, but the Harlem Hellfighters had done their part.

DESEGREGATING THE MILITARY

In July 1948, President Harry S. Truman issued Executive Order 9981, which prohibited racial and ethnic discrimination in the military. Prior to this time, black members of the armed services served in separate units from white troops. Even after Truman's executive order, integration was not implemented because of white opposition. But during the Korean War, US Major General W. B. Kean placed approximately 250 black enlisted men with each white regiment. Kean reported morale was good and in "many instances close friendships developed."[7] In 1953, the army abolished the last all-black military units, ending the practice of segregation.

TIMELINE

June 28, 1914

War is sparked by the assassination of Archduke Ferdinand and his wife.

July 28, 1914

Austria-Hungary declares war on Serbia. World War I begins.

June 1916

Enlistment begins in New York for the Fifteenth New York National Guard Regiment.

April 6, 1917

The United States declares war on Germany.

March 21, 1918

The Fifteenth New York National Guard Regiment begins training under French command.

May 15, 1918

Henry Johnson and Needham Roberts withstand a German attack.

September 26, 1918

The Meuse-Argonne Offensive begins.

November 11, 1918

Germany surrenders and signs an armistice.

June 15, 1917

The Fifteenth New York National Guard Regiment reaches combat strength with more than 2,000 men.

October 8, 1917

The Fifteenth transfers to Spartanburg, South Carolina, amid great racial tension.

December 27, 1917

The Fifteenth arrives in Brest, France.

March 3, 1918

Russia and Germany sign a separate peace treaty, ending Russia's involvement in the war.

December 17, 1918

The 369th is released from French service.

February 12, 1919

The 369th arrives back in New York.

February 17, 1919

A victory parade is held in New York City for the 369th.

July 1948

President Harry S. Truman issues Executive Order 9981, prohibiting racial and ethnic discrimination in the military.

ESSENTIAL FACTS

KEY PLAYERS

- Colonel William Hayward was the white commanding officer of the Fifteenth New York National Guard Regiment, the "Harlem Hellfighters."

- General John J. Pershing was commander of all US forces during World War I.

- James Reese Europe was the African-American leader of the Fifteenth regimental band, which toured France to great acclaim and helped popularize jazz in France.

- General Henri Gouraud was the French general of the Fourth Army, under whose leadership the 369th served.

KEY EVENTS

On July 28, 1914, Austria-Hungary declares war on Serbia and World War I begins. Colonel William Hayward, the white commander of the all-black Fifteenth New York National Guard Regiment, begins enlisting men in June 1916. The Fifteenth arrives in France on December 27, 1917, and General John J. Pershing ultimately decides to have them fight as part of the French army. The Fifteenth New York National Guard Regiment is renamed the 369th US Infantry and begins training with the French on March 21, 1918. The men of the 369th are the first African-American troops in World War I combat. Throughout their time in France, they will fight as part of the French force and earn the nickname "Harlem Hellfighters" for their fighting skills. After Germany surrenders, the 369th is released from French service on December 17, 1918. They return to the United States and are honored as heroes during a victory parade in New York City on February 17, 1919.

IMPACT ON SOCIETY

In Europe, the devastating effects of World War I ultimately paved the way for World War II. In the United States, the effect of World War I on African Americans was significant. The war sped up the Great Migration. It increased the pride and prestige of African-American soldiers and the black community in general. Men came home from the war more committed than ever to fighting for racial equality and justice, not only in the United States but internationally as well. The sense of black pride and action also contributed to the rise of the cultural movement known as the Harlem Renaissance. Although the number of black soldiers in combat and leadership slowly increased, official military segregation continued until 1948.

QUOTE

"As anyone who recalls the assurances of 1917 and 1918, I confess personally a deep sense of disappointment of poignant pain, that a great country in time of need should promise so much and afterward perform so little."

—*Emmett Scott, assistant to Secretary of War Newton Baker*

GLOSSARY

ABOLITIONIST
A person who wants to end slavery.

ARMISTICE
A temporary stop of fighting by mutual agreement.

ARTILLERY
Large guns manned by a crew of operators used to shoot long distances.

BAYONET
A swordlike blade attached to the end of a rifle.

CIVILIAN
A person not serving in the armed forces.

DISCRIMINATION
Unfair treatment of other people, usually because of race, age, or gender.

FLANK
The right or left side of a military formation.

FRONT
An area where a battle is taking place.

INDUSTRIALIZATION
The process of changing a culture from mainly an agricultural economy to one that manufactures goods.

INFANTRY
Soldiers who fight on foot; the branch of the army including these soldiers.

NATIONAL GUARD
A state military force kept in reserve for times of emergency.

OFFENSIVE
Large-scale attack against the enemy.

REGIMENT
An army unit typically commanded by a colonel.

SEGREGATION
The practice of separating groups of people based on race, gender, ethnicity, or other factors.

SNIPER
An infantry rifleman whose task is to kill individual enemy soldiers at long range.

ADDITIONAL RESOURCES

SELECTED BIBLIOGRAPHY

Harris, Stephen L. *Harlem's Hell Fighters: The African-American 369th Infantry in World War I.* Washington, DC: Brassey's, 2003. Print.

Nelson, Peter N. *A More Unbending Battle: The Harlem Hellfighters' Struggle for Freedom in WWI and Equality at Home.* New York: BasicCivitas, 2009. Print.

Sweeney, W. Allison. *History of the American Negro in the Great World War.* New York: Johnson Reprint, 1970. Print.

Wright, Ben. "Victory and Defeat: World War I, the Harlem Hellfighters, and a Lost Battle for Civil Rights." *Afro-Americans in New York Life and History* 38.1 (2014). *EBSCOHost.* Web. 19 Apr. 2015.

FURTHER READINGS

Brooks, Max. *Harlem Hellfighters.* New York: Crown, 2014. Print.

Grant, R. G. *World War I: The Definitive Visual Guide.* London: DK, 2014. Print.

Pratt, Mary K. *World War I.* Minneapolis: ABDO, 2014. Print.

WEBSITES

To learn more about Essential Library of World War I, visit **booklinks.abdopublishing.com**. These links are routinely monitored and updated to provide the most current information available.

PLACES TO VISIT

The National Museum of African American History and Culture
1400 Constitution Avenue, NW
Washington, DC 20004
202-633-1000
http://nmaahc.si.edu/
Scheduled to open in 2016, the Smithsonian National Museum of African American History and Culture is under construction on the National Mall in Washington, DC. The museum will be a place where all Americans can learn about the richness and diversity of the African-American experience and how it helped shape the United States. Until the museum opens, visitors can tour the MAAHC gallery located in the Smithsonian National Museum of American History.

National World War I Museum at Liberty Memorial
100 W. Twenty-Sixth Street
Kansas City, MO 64108
816-888-8100
http://www.theworldwar.org
The National World War I Museum at Liberty Memorial is the only American museum dedicated solely to World War I. With one of the greatest collections of World War I artifacts anywhere in the world, the museum uses its world-class collection, along with interactive technology, to tell the story of the war through the eyes of those who lived it.

SOURCE NOTES

CHAPTER 1. BATTLING BLACK DEATH

1. Ben Wright. "Victory and Defeat: World War I, the Harlem Hellfighters, and a Lost Battle for Civil Rights." *Afro-Americans in New York Life and History* 38.1 (2014). *EBSCOHost*. Web. 19 Apr. 2015.

2. Gilbert King. "Remembering Henry Johnson, the Soldier Called 'Black Death.'" *Smithsonian.com*. Smithsonian Institute, 25 Oct. 2011. Web. 11 May 2015.

3. Peter N. Nelson. *A More Unbending Battle: The Harlem Hellfighters' Struggle for Freedom in WWI and Equality at Home*. New York: BasicCivitas, 2009. Print. 104–109.

4. "The Harlem Hellfighters: The Most Storied African-American Combat Unit of World War I." *abmc.gov*. American Battle Monuments Commission, n.d. Web. 9 Apr. 2015.

5. "369th Infantry Regiment World War One." *New York State Military Museum and Veterans Research Center*. NYS Division of Military and Naval Affairs, n.d. Web. 9 Apr. 2015.

CHAPTER 2. THE FIGHT FOR FREEDOM

1. Kevin D. Roberts. "Demographics." *Encyclopedia of African American History, 1619–1895*. Ed. Paul Finkelman. New York: Oxford UP, 2008. *Oxford African American Studies Center*. Web. 25 Apr. 2015.

2. Mariana Candido, et al. "Slave Trade." *Encyclopedia of African American History, 1619–1895*. Ed. Paul Finkelman. New York: Oxford UP, 2008. *Oxford African American Studies Center*. Web. 5 May 2015.

3. "American Revolution." *Africana: The Encyclopedia of the African and African American Experience*. Ed. Kwame Anthony Appiah, et al. New York: Oxford UP, 2008. *Oxford African American Studies Center*. Web. 28 Apr. 2015.

4. Douglas R. Egerton. "American Revolution." *Encyclopedia of African American History, 1619–1895*. Ed. Paul Finkelman. New York: Oxford UP, 2008. *Oxford African American Studies Center*. Web. 5 May 2015.

5. Arnold Rampersad. "The Souls of Black Folk." *The Concise Oxford Companion to African American Literature*. Ed. William L. Andrews, et al. New York: Oxford UP, 2008. *Oxford African American Studies Center*. Web. 30 Apr. 2015.

6. Gordon Morris Bakken. "Military." *Encyclopedia of African American History, 1619–1895*. Ed. Paul Finkelman. New York: Oxford UP, 2008. *Oxford African American Studies Center*. Web. 1 May 2015.

7. "Timeline." *Oxford African American Studies Center*, n.d. Web. 18 Apr. 2015.

8. Gordon Morris Bakken. "Military." Encyclopedia of African American History, 1619-1895. Ed. Paul Finkelman. New York: Oxford UP, 2008. Oxford African American Studies Center. Web. 1 May 2015.

CHAPTER 3. FIGHTING FOR EQUALITY ON THE HOME FRONT

1. Kevin D. Roberts. "Demographics." *Encyclopedia of African American History, 1619–1895*. Ed. Paul Finkelman. New York: Oxford UP, 2008. *Oxford African American Studies Center*. Web. 25 Apr. 2015.

2. Cary D. Wintz. "World War I." *Encyclopedia of African American History, 1896 to the Present*. Ed. Paul Finkelman. New York: Oxford UP, 2008. *Oxford African American Studies Center*. Web. 27 Apr. 2015.

3. "African Americans and World War I." *Africana Age*. Schomburg Center for Research in Black Culture, n.d. Web. 26 Apr. 2015.

4. Peter N. Nelson. *A More Unbending Battle: The Harlem Hellfighters' Struggle for Freedom in WWI and Equality at Home*. New York: BasicCivitas, 2009. Print. 4.

5. "World War I." *Europe Since 1914: Encyclopedia of the Age of War and Reconstruction*. Ed. John Merriman, et al. Vol. 5. Detroit: Charles Scribner's Sons, 2006. 2751–2766. *World History in Context*. Web. 9 May 2015.

6. Stephen L. Harris. *Harlem's Hell Fighters: The African-American 369th Infantry in World War I*. Washington, DC: Brassey's, 2003. Print. 33.

7. Ibid. 31.

CHAPTER 4. RECRUITING THE FIGHTING FIFTEENTH

1. Stephen L. Harris. *Harlem's Hell Fighters: The African-American 369th Infantry in World War I*. Washington, DC: Brassey's, 2003. Print. 30.

2. Emmett J. Scott. *Scott's Official History of the American Negro in the World War*. Chicago: Homewood, 1919. Print. 197.

3. Ibid.

4. Stephen L. Harris. *Harlem's Hell Fighters: The African-American 369th Infantry in World War I*. Washington, DC: Brassey's, 2003. Print. 43.

5. Ibid. 71.

6. Peter N. Nelson. *A More Unbending Battle: The Harlem Hellfighters' Struggle for Freedom in WWI and Equality at Home*. New York: BasicCivitas, 2009. Print. 21.

7. James Sellman. "World War I and African Americans." *Africana: The Encyclopedia of the African and African American Experience*. Ed. Kwame Anthony Appiah, et al. New York: Oxford UP, 2008. *Oxford African American Studies Center*. Web. 30 Apr. 2015.

8. Peter N. Nelson. *A More Unbending Battle: The Harlem Hellfighters' Struggle for Freedom in WWI and Equality at Home*. New York: BasicCivitas, 2009. Print. 21.

9. Ben Wright. "Victory and Defeat: World War I, the Harlem Hellfighters, and a Lost Battle for Civil Rights." *Afro-Americans in New York Life and History* 38.1 (2014). *EBSCOHost*. Web. 19 Apr. 2015.

10. Stephen L. Harris. *Harlem's Hell Fighters: The African-American 369th Infantry in World War I*. Washington, DC: Brassey's, 2003. Print. 97.

11. Debora Duerksen. "Harlem Hell Fighters." *Encyclopedia of African American History, 1896 to the Present*. Ed. Paul Finkelman. New York: Oxford UP, 2008. *Oxford African American Studies Center*. Web. 30 Apr. 2015.

12. "The Use of Poison Gases in the First World War." *Science and Its Times*. Ed. Neil Schlager, et al. Vol. 6. Detroit: Gale, 2001. *World History in Context*. Web. 9 May 2015.

CHAPTER 5. WAR IN EUROPE AND WAR AT HOME

1. Ben Wright. "Victory and Defeat: World War I, the Harlem Hellfighters, and a Lost Battle for Civil Rights." *Afro-Americans in New York Life and History* 38.1 (2014). *EBSCOHost*. Web. 19 Apr. 2015.

2. Chad L. Williams. "Vanguards of the New Negro: African American Veterans and Post-World War I Racial Militancy."

SOURCE NOTES
CONTINUED

The Journal of African American History 92.3 (2007). *JSTOR*. Web. 4 July 2015.

3. Cary D. Wintz. "World War I." *Encyclopedia of African American History, 1896 to the Present*. Ed. Paul Finkelman. New York: Oxford UP, 2008. *Oxford African American Studies Center*. Web. 27 Apr. 2015.

4. Alonford James. Robinson. "East St. Louis Riot of 1917." *Africana: The Encyclopedia of the African and African American Experience*. Ed. Kwame Anthony Appiah, et al. New York: Oxford UP, 2008. *Oxford African American Studies Center*. Web. 1 May 2015.

5. Peter N. Nelson. *A More Unbending Battle: The Harlem Hellfighters' Struggle for Freedom in WWI and Equality at Home*. New York: BasicCivitas, 2009. Print. 31.

6. Gordon Morris Bakken. "Military." *Encyclopedia of African American History, 1619–1895*. Ed. Paul Finkelman. New York: Oxford UP, 2008. *Oxford African American Studies Center*. Web. 1 May 2015.

7. Maggi M. Morehouse. "Racism in the Military." *Encyclopedia of African American History, 1896 to the Present*. Ed. Paul Finkelman. New York: Oxford UP, 2008. *Oxford African American Studies Center*. Web. 2 May 2015.

8. Peter N. Nelson. *A More Unbending Battle: The Harlem Hellfighters' Struggle for Freedom in WWI and Equality at Home*. New York: BasicCivitas, 2009. Print. 35.

9. Stephen L. Harris. *Harlem's Hell Fighters: The African-American 369th Infantry in World War I*. Washington, DC: Brassey's, 2003. Print. 122.

CHAPTER 6. THE FIGHTING FIFTEENTH IN FRANCE

1. Stephen L. Harris. *Harlem's Hell Fighters: The African-American 369th Infantry in World War I*. Washington, DC: Brassey's, 2003. Print. 159.

2. Ibid. 164.

3. Maggi M. Morehouse. "Racism in the Military." *Encyclopedia of African American History, 1896 to the Present*. Ed. Paul Finkelman. New York: Oxford UP, 2008. *Oxford African American Studies Center*. Web. 2 May 2015.

4. Stephen L. Harris. *Harlem's Hell Fighters: The African-American 369th Infantry in World War I*. Washington, DC: Brassey's, 2003. Print. 178.

5. Ibid.

6. Ibid. 179.

7. Peter N. Nelson. *A More Unbending Battle: The Harlem Hellfighters' Struggle for Freedom in WWI and Equality at Home*. New York: BasicCivitas, 2009. Print. 72.

8. Ibid. 62.

CHAPTER 7. AT THE FRONT

1. "Army Units and Sizes." *Second World War*. Secondworldwar.co.uk, n.d. Web. 27 Apr. 2015.

2. Maggi M. Morehouse. "Racism in the Military." *Encyclopedia of African American History, 1896 to the Present*. Ed. Paul Finkelman. New York: Oxford UP, 2008. *Oxford African American Studies Center*. Web. 2 May 2015.

3. Debora Duerksen. "Harlem Hell Fighters." *Encyclopedia of African American History, 1896 to the Present*. Ed. Paul Finkelman. New York: Oxford UP, 2008. *Oxford African American Studies Center*. Web. 30 Apr. 2015.

4. Stephen L. Harris. *Harlem's Hell Fighters: The African-American 369th Infantry in World War I*. Washington, DC: Brassey's, 2003. Print. 205–209.

5. Ibid. 121.

6. Ibid. 221.

7. Bill Harris. *The Hellfighters of Harlem: African-American Soldiers Who Fought for the Right to Fight for Their Country.* New York: Carroll & Graf, 2002. Print. 38.

8. Gordon Morris Bakken. "Military." *Encyclopedia of African American History, 1619–1895.* Ed. Paul Finkelman. New York: Oxford UP, 2008. *Oxford African American Studies Center.* Web. 1 May 2015.

9. Ben Wright. "Victory and Defeat: World War I, the Harlem Hellfighters, and a Lost Battle for Civil Rights." *Afro-Americans in New York Life and History* 38.1 (2014). *EBSCOHost.* Web. 19 Apr. 2015.

10. Ibid.

CHAPTER 8. THE BOYS COME HOME

1. W. Allison Sweeney. *History of the American Negro in the Great World War.* New York: Johnson Reprint, 1970. Print. 267.

2. Henry Louis Gates Jr. "Who Were the Harlem Hellfighters?" *The African Americans.* PBS, n.d. Web. 18 Apr. 2015.

3. W. Allison Sweeney. *History of the American Negro in the Great World War.* New York: Johnson Reprint, 1970. Print. 270.

4. Bill Harris. *The Hellfighters of Harlem: African-American Soldiers Who Fought for the Right to Fight for Their Country.* New York: Carroll & Graf, 2002. Print.

5. W. Allison Sweeney. *History of the American Negro in the Great World War.* New York: Johnson Reprint, 1970. Print. 273.

CHAPTER 9. AFTERMATH OF BIRACIAL WARFARE

1. Cary D. Wintz. "World War I." *Encyclopedia of African American History, 1896 to the Present.* Ed. Paul Finkelman. New York: Oxford UP, 2008. *Oxford African American Studies Center.* Web. 27 Apr. 2015.

2. Peter N. Nelson. *A More Unbending Battle: The Harlem Hellfighters' Struggle for Freedom in WWI and Equality at Home.* New York: BasicCivitas, 2009. Print. 61.

3. Ben Wright. "Victory and Defeat: World War I, the Harlem Hellfighters, and a Lost Battle for Civil Rights." *Afro-Americans in New York Life and History* 38.1 (2014). *EBSCOHost.* Web. 19 Apr. 2015.

4. Cary D. Wintz. "World War I." *Encyclopedia of African American History, 1896 to the Present.* Ed. Paul Finkelman. New York: Oxford UP, 2008. *Oxford African American Studies Center.* Web. 27 Apr. 2015.

5. Gordon Morris Bakken. "Military." *Encyclopedia of African American History, 1619–1895.* Ed. Paul Finkelman. New York: Oxford UP, 2008. *Oxford African American Studies Center.* Web. 1 May 2015.

6. Ron E. Armstead. "Veterans in the Fight for Equal Rights: From the Civil War to Today." *Trotter Review* 18.1.12 (2009): 97. Web. 15 Apr. 2015.

7. Sherie Mershon and Steven Schlossman. *Foxholes & Color Lines: Desegregating the U.S. Armed Forces.* Baltimore: Johns Hopkins UP, 1998. Print. 226.

INDEX

ABOUT THE AUTHOR

Shannon Baker Moore is a freelance writer and editor who writes for both adults and children. A college writing instructor and writing coach, Shannon is a member of SCBWI (Society of Children's Book Writers & Illustrators). Author of *The Korean War* (Essential Library of American Wars series), *King Tut's Tomb* (Digging Up the Past series), and *A History of Music* (Essential Library of Cultural History series), Shannon blogs about children's books at http://www.greatbooksforchildren.com. She and her family have lived throughout the United States and currently call Saint Louis, Missouri, home.